WALL

templar books
an imprint of Candlewick Press

My mom said that while the wall was being made,

our dad got stuck on the other side.

I worried he was lonely,

but Mom said life was better over there.

And we couldn't leave, anyway.

I dreamed of Dad breaking through the wall and rescuing us.

But I knew
that my dreams
were unlikely to come true.

Still, I imagined
all kinds of ways
to get across.

Many people did try to escape—

in all kinds of inventive ways.

While some were lucky,
others were not.

But if we never tried,
we might never see Dad again.

So I started
digging.

Finally, when the tunnel was
ready, we left that night.

The hardest part was crossing the field to the tunnel's entrance undetected.

We were stopped
by a thunderous
voice calling

"HALT!"

The soldier asked us what we were doing,

so I told him about my dad.

He said nothing should come between a father and his family,

and he let us go

We headed through the crowds...

to a small house on a quiet street.

We were just in time.

This book was typeset in Brown. The illustrations were created digitally.

TEMPLAR BOOKS, an imprint of Candlewick Press, 99 Dover Street,
Somerville, Massachusetts 02144. www.candlewick.com

Printed in Dongguan, Guangdong, China
14 15 16 17 18 19 TLF 10 9 8 7 6 5 4 3 2 1